D1377744

Love You Always

Written by Eileen Spinelli
Illustrated by Gillian Flint

ISBN-13: 978-0-8249-5686-8

Published by WorthyKids/Ideals
An imprint of Worthy Publishing Group
A division of Worthy Media, Inc.
Nashville, Tennessee

Library of Congress CIP data on file

Designed by Eve DeGrie

Printed and bound in China
RRD-SZ_Jun17_1

For our latest "greats": Mason, Christian, Luca, Greyson, Anthony, Zac, and Kassiana . . . Love you always. —E.S.

For Simon, for always believing in me,
and for Owen and Thea, who inspire me daily. —G.F.

This book is for

Seasons come
and seasons go.

Mama loves you always.

Sometimes rain

and sometimes snow.

Mama loves you always.

You can giggle,
cry, or pout,
but you are loved
without a doubt,

upside-down and
inside-out!

Mama loves you always.

Daddy loves you always.

Loves you silly.

Loves you sad.

Loves you naughty.

Loves you mad.

Loves you *two*, *four*,
six, *eight*, *ten* . . .
to the moon and
back again!

Daddy loves you always.

Grandma loves you always.

Loves you dancing—

tap,

tap,

tap.

Loves you singing—

clap,

clap,

clap.

Loves you napping on her lap.

Grandma loves you always.

Grandpa loves you always too.

Loves you playing peek-a-boo
in the park . . .

or at the zoo.

Grandpa loves you always.

Auntie loves you. You're her joy.
She helps you find your favorite toy.

TOY

Uncle loves you,

swings you high

like an airplane in the sky.

Cousin calls you Doodlebug.

Family friend gives you a hug,
brings you books of poetry.

Sweet leaf on
the family tree,
you are steeped
in love like tea.

Always.
Always.

Always.